STAGE FRIGHT

by Erica David

Illustrated by Victoria Miller

and Harry Moore

SCHOLASTIC INC.

New York   Toronto   London   Auckland   Sydney
Mexico City   New Delhi   Hong Kong   Buenos Aires

© 2005 Viacom International Inc. All Rights Reserved.
Nickelodeon, Danny Phantom and all related titles,
logos and characters are trademarks of Viacom International Inc.

No part of this publication may be reproduced in whole or in part,
or stored in a retrieval system, or transmitted in any form or
by any means, electronic, mechanical, photocopying, recording,
or otherwise, without written permission of the publisher.

Published by Scholastic Inc.,
90 Old Sherman Turnpike, Danbury, Connecticut 06816.

SCHOLASTIC and associated logos are trademarks
and/or registered trademarks of Scholastic Inc.

ISBN 0-439-78278-3

First Scholastic Printing, October 2005

CHAPTERS

"Good news, class," said Mr. Lancer, the English teacher at Casper High School. "We're going to put on a production of William Shakespeare's *Macbeth*."

SHAKESPEARE'S MACBETH
CLASS Production

Danny Fenton turned to his friend Tucker Foley and groaned. "Great," he whispered. "Whenever we read Shakespeare I get completely lost."

"I've noticed that, Fenton, which is why I'm giving you the part of Macbeth," announced Mr. Lancer.

"*What?*" Danny cried.

"It's the lead role so you'll have to study the play very carefully," Mr. Lancer explained. "There'll be no chance of you getting lost."

"It won't be so bad, Danny," said his friend Samantha Manson.

"There is one more thing I should mention, class," said Mr. Lancer. "This play is cursed!"

"What do you mean cursed?" asked Tucker.

"It's an old theater superstition. You can't say the name of the play once rehearsals begin or bad things will start to happen," Mr. Lancer replied.

"Sounds creepy," said Sam.

"Sounds like my life just took a turn for the worse," Danny groaned.

CHAPTER 2
A POOR PLAYER

A few days later, Danny and his friends met up at the school auditorium.

"Have you practiced your lines?" asked Sam.

"I haven't had time," answered Danny.
"Every time I sit down to memorize my
lines, some ghost decides to get his
haunt on."

"Let's begin," Mr. Lancer announced. "We'll start with You-Know-Who's speech at the end of act 1."

"Who's this You-Know-Who?" Danny whispered to Sam.

"You are," she replied.

"No, I'm not," Danny said. "Lancer made me Mac—"

"Don't say it!" Tucker cut him off.
"Remember the curse!"

"Right, the curse. How could I forget?"
Danny sighed. He walked up onstage and
took his place in the center.

"Whenever you're ready, Fenton," Mr.
Lancer told him.

Danny cleared his throat. "If it were done . . . when 'tis done, wherefore uh, whither be thee . . . my fine feathered friend," he finished lamely.

"Well, Danny, it's obvious you haven't been studying the play," Mr. Lancer stated.

"I'm sorry," Danny apologized. "I've just been really busy after school."

"Listen, Fenton, if you don't learn your lines on your own time, you'll have to do it during detention in my office," Mr. Lancer said. "Understand?"

"Yes, sir," Danny muttered.

Danny walked offstage to where Sam and Tucker were waiting for him. "I'll never have time to learn this!" he grumbled.

"Just relax," said Sam. "Tucker and I will help you with your lines after school."

"It isn't just the lines! The more time I spend at rehearsal, the less time I have to catch ghosts!" Danny shouted.

"Shhh! Calm down, someone might hear you," Tucker advised.

"I will *not* calm down. I wish I'd never heard of stupid Macbeth in the first place!" yelled Danny.

Tucker and Sam gasped in shock.

"What?" Danny snapped.

"You just said the *M*-word,"
Sam explained.

"You've unleashed the curse!"
cried Tucker.

"I did some research on this curse thing last night. We're doomed!" Sam declared at lunch the next day.

"We aren't doomed,"
Danny said. "The curse
is bogus."

"That's what some people say
about ghosts," Tucker replied.

"Don't tell me you're taking this
seriously?" asked Danny.

Sam and Tucker shrugged.

After school that day, Danny's class gathered for another rehearsal. While a group of students worked on the set, Sam practiced one of her scenes as a witch.

"Scale of dragon, tooth of wolf . . . " Sam began. But she stopped suddenly when a bucket of paint fell from a ladder and spilled all over Danny.

"Are you okay, Danny?" asked Sam, trying not to laugh.

"Just peachy," Danny spluttered.

"That was totally bizarre," Sam said. "I mean, there was no one near that can of paint."

"It's the curse!" exclaimed Tucker.

"It is not!" Danny insisted.

"Well, how do you explain it then?"
Tucker challenged.

"It's just another humiliating event in
my high school career," Danny replied.

The next week, another strange thing happened at play rehearsal. Tucker was helping Danny to practice his lines when they heard a mysterious creaking noise. Suddenly one of the spotlights broke from the ceiling!

Danny grabbed Tucker and used his
ghost powers to make them both intangible.
The light passed right through them and
hit the ground with a crash.

Mr. Lancer ran backstage. "Is everyone all right?" he asked.

"Yes," Danny answered quickly. "Nothing to see here. We'll just go back to running lines."

After Mr. Lancer left, Tucker opened his mouth to speak.

"Not a word," Danny cut him off. "There is *no* curse."

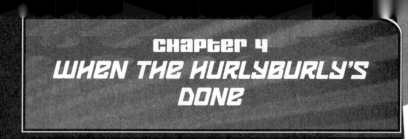

CHAPTER 4
WHEN THE HURLYBURLY'S DONE

On opening night a few weeks later,
Danny, Sam, and Tucker met backstage.

"I can't wait until this is over," Danny said. "I'm completely fried. I've been up every night for weeks memorizing lines."

"We know, we were there," Tucker reminded him.

I know," Danny replied. "You two are the reason I'm a lean, mean Shakespeare machine. Thanks, guys."

"No problem," Tucker answered.

"I've got good news," Sam said. "According to the Internet, when the play ends we'll finally be free of the curse!"

"For the last time there is no curse!" Danny shouted.

"You have to admit that some weird things have been happening around here," Sam persisted. "Like that day when all the props disappeared."

Or the time the witches' cauldron exploded," added Tucker.

"Or the day the curtain attacked you?" Sam finished.

"Look, guys, it isn't a—" Danny stopped
short as a puff of ghost breath escaped his
lips. *That only happens when there's a
ghost nearby*, he thought.

"That's it!" Danny exclaimed. "It isn't a curse. But it *is* a ghost!"

He quickly transformed to use his ghost powers to investigate.

Just then a heavy piece
of scenery began to wobble.

"Danny, behind you!"
Sam cried.

As the set piece began to tip over, Danny flew over and braced himself against it. He used all of his strength to push it back into place.

"That was a close one!" Tucker exclaimed.

"Not nearly close enough!" hissed a mysterious voice.

A stately ghost floated out from behind the scenery. "Allow me to introduce myself," he said. "I am Sir Milton Hamalot, the true star of this play!"

"So you're responsible for all those weird accidents!" Danny accused the ghost.

"Precisely," Sir Hamalot confirmed.

"But why?" asked Danny.

"Why, you ask? I am an *actor*," Sir Hamalot intoned. "I know that must be difficult for a cut-rate thespian, such as yourself, to understand."

"What did he call me?" Danny whispered to Tucker.

"After all of these long years
haunting the halls of this amateur theater,
finally there's a production worthy of my
talent," explained Sir Hamalot.

"Yet once again I was passed over for the lead role!" Sir Hamalot roared.

"Wait a minute," said Danny. "You mean you want my part?"

Sir Hamalot. "I deserve the role of Macbeth!
I know every single line in the play!"

"Yeah?" Danny said. "Prove it."

"Nave! Dost thou challenge me to a duel of words?" asked Sir Hamalot.

"I dost . . . uh . . . do . . . " answered Danny.

"Very well, you first," Sir Hamalot announced, "act 1, scene 7."

*I know this
one*, Danny thought,
remembering the lines. *This guy is
toast!* "If it were done when 'tis
done, then 'twere well it were done
quickly," he quoted. "Your turn, act 2,
scene 1."

"Is this a dagger which I see before me, the handle toward my hand?" Sir Hamalot recited. Keeping the ghost busy delivering lines from the play, Danny quietly slipped the Fenton Thermos from his pocket.

"Your turn," Sir Hamalot cried, "act 3, scene 2."

"Go thou, ghost, into this thermos and get thee gone!" Danny snarled.

"That isn't a line from the play!"
Sir Hamalot howled, as he was
sucked into the thermos.

"You're right," Danny replied.
"That's a Fenton original."

Danny transformed back into his human self. "Well, I guess we all learned an important lesson here tonight," he said.

"Beware of theater ghosts?" Tucker asked.

"Always study your lines?" Sam suggested.

"Nobody upstages Danny Fenton," answered Danny.

Mr. Lancer ran backstage to check on
his cast. "Places everyone. We're on in
5 minutes," he announced. "And Fenton,
you'd better know your lines."

"Fear thee not, Mr. Lancer," Danny said.
"I'm an *actor*. I knoweth every single one."